From the Icy Fingers of the Deep

Sea Tales by Chris Kastle

ISBN: 978-0-9887553-3-8

Cover art: original watercolor copyright © 2014 by Chris Kastle

Photo of Chris Kastle by Joyce Sabato, Copyright © 2011 by Chris Kastle

Cover and interior layout and design by Jonni Anderson jonnianderson.com; starwatchcreations.com

Edited by: Robert G. Mankin

Sons of Aaron Publishing
Palm Coast, Florida

Acknowledgements

Thank you to my editor, Robert G. Makin, author of *The Faces of Innana, Strathnaver Legends, Aleister through the Looking Glass*, and *Return to Masada*.

Thanks and fair winds to Captain Tom Kelly, who founded the Inland Seas Education Association and introduced me to the alien monsters of the Great Lakes.

Special thanks to my brother, Dr. William Rabiega for his excellent advice and mentoring, to my good friends Pam Linder and Joyce Sabato for their enthusiasm and support, and to my extended family the Tale Tellers of St. Augustine for helping to keep the art of storytelling alive.

This book is dedicated with great affection to a fine storyteller, helpmate, and second mother, Shirley Bryce.

Contents

Forward

How enticing it is to contemplate the beauty and treachery of the endless ocean, vast, mysterious, and yet unconquered. Water is the essence of life. It draws us from within and without. Even more fascinating is the possibility of things unreal that lurk at the edge of the horizon in the uncertain places of the imagination — the place where the mind meets the sea.

I have enjoyed exploring that place through the stories included in this book. Some came purely out of the ethers and took their own paths to the end of the tale. Others were inspired by existing legend, myth, fairytale, folklore and also by historical fact. It has been exciting and challenging to cast a net into my own creativity and harvest such a diverse catch.

Daughter of the Wind

The wind called to her. How she longed to go out in the boats with her older sister and brothers, with her father. She longed to take the tiller and ride the waves and catch the fish, but she was only eleven. It would be two more years before she was allowed. Sometimes on warm days in light air when the breeze blew pleasantly, one of her siblings would take her out on the skiff for a short sail along the shore and she would thrill to the gentle pressure of the air as it pressed against the canvas and touched her face. She heard it whisper sweet lullabies.

On days when the wind blew with great force, she would go down to the shore and let it whip her hair and wrap its invisible arms around her. She drew in its power with every breath. One day she would sail in such weather! But now she must continue to gather the seaweed from the tidal pools and fill the basket woven of palm fronds. It was to be part of the fish stew that she would help her mother make for their evening meal. At least it brought her down to the shore where she and the wind could talk.

Although her mother told the old family stories and taught her how to weave and cook and repair the nets, the girl knew that she was born to be at sea — a true daughter of the wind. Once or twice she tried to tell her mother, who just told her to wait for her time. Her mother would also tell her stories about the time before she was married and had children, the time when she worked the water and lowered the nets and helped to haul in the harvest — a harvest of slippery silver fish that flipped and flapped as they poured into the bottom of the boat. She heard of the golden sunrises that brought good fortune and of the red ones that did not. She heard about the flying fish that glided above the water with their large pectoral fins. She heard about the strong currents and the tides and the storms — of how the wind could be calm one minute and blow brutally strong the next. Of course, all of these stories were meant to help her prepare for when she got older. Getting older wasn't happening fast enough for her! She stirred the stew and fed the fire. The wind was silent when she did this, and it made her feel empty.

At sunset, the fishers returned. Everyone helped to bring the fleet to shore and secure the vessels with heavy woven ropes. Those who had been waiting ashore welcomed their friends and family with open arms to safety. They all admired the catch. There were many baskets of fish, but the fish were smaller than usual. The crews had prepared the fish as they were caught. The roe was gathered and the offal thrown back to the sea to feed many creatures. Nothing was wasted.

The next morning the sun peaked above the horizon in a crimson hue. The girl went down to the shore to catch the first movement of air just as it started to build with the beginning of the day. She peered out across the water and then she noticed that one of the boats had broken free during the night and was floating slowly towards the open sea. It would be a great loss to her community and she knew she should run and tell her mother and father. But, just then, a very small puff of breeze found its way into her ear and it put a thought into her head. *What if I swim out and bring the boat back? There is barely any air movement and the water is calm. I am an excellent swimmer. I could be a hero!* So persuasive was that little puff that the girl forgot all of the teachings of her mother, she forgot all of the warnings that were part of the fabric of her heritage, and she waded out into the water until it got too deep to stand and then she swam. She swam long easy strokes — it wouldn't be far now. Yet every time she thought she was getting closer, the boat seemed to be farther than she thought. Distances on the water can be deceiving. She was starting to get tired, she was starting to think that she was not going to be any kind of hero, but, instead, drown at sea and when she looked toward the land it was, indeed, a long way off. She started to see a vision, then, of her lifeless form washed up on the beach, pale and still, her hair twisted with sponges and seaweed. Her family and friends shuddered with grief. It was her mother that found her, the girl could see her mother's salt tears falling on her daughter's face and mixing with the salt that already encrusted it.

Just then something bumped into her, it was the boat. She hoisted herself inside and breathed a sigh of relief. She rested only a short while because she knew that as the sun rose, it would become hotter and the wind would continue to build. And, also, she did not bring any fresh water to drink or food to eat. Not wasting any time, the girl stepped the small mast and set the sail — for home. It was not fast enough. The sun had already shared its warmth with the sea so that the wind and the waves and the clouds grew high. The land was now only a thin strip to be seen between the mountains of rolling water. The rain started to fall and she didn't know where the land was anymore. The ever increasing wind cradled her as it sang sweet songs in the rigging, and she closed her eyes.

In the morning, she awoke to a sunrise that was the color of lemons and a breeze that would surely take her home. She set a course away from the light, for she knew the direction of home. After a while she could see her familiar shore. She could see her people gathered and waiting there to greet her and praise her heroic act. But as her friend, the wind, pulled her closer to the coast, she noticed that no one was looking seaward to greet her. Instead, they were looking at something on the beach. No one helped her to bring the boat out of the water, but somehow she managed to do it all alone. Why *didn't* they help her?

The girl was confused and cold and tired and didn't understand, but when she walked over to where they had gathered and looked at what they were all seeing, she knew why. She saw her own body, pale and still, her hair twisted with sponges and seaweed. Her family and friends shuddered with grief. It was her mother that found her. The girl could see her mother's salt tears falling on her daughter's face and mixing with the salt that already encrusted it. She saw the broken tiller clutched in her stiffened little hand.

She heard the wind as it spun around her. She felt herself whirl as she moved with it. And as it embraced her, she became one with the wind.

Blackbeard: Born to Be a Pirate

Edward Teach or Thatch or Tach or maybe Edward Drummond, who most know as Blackbeard — was a man born to be a pirate. He is the stuff of which legends are made — and he was no slacker in creating the legend that lives on to this very day. It was his habit to be heavily armed. He let his thick, black beard grow untamed and untrimmed. He wove fuses into this beard and lit them just before going into battle. Of course the fuses were soaked in fat to burn slowly and smoke but not flame. Sometimes he would also tie red ribbons among the fuses.

He began his seafaring career working on a British Privateer during the War of Spanish Succession. With that over in 1713, he turned to piracy, but did not come into his own until he was given command of his own ship in 1716 when he became one of the most efficient and effective, ever, at the business of piracy. Piracy was and still is a business. Back then, people often viewed it as quite an attractive option during bad times. In several colonies, public officials considered it to be a means of commerce and survival for residents. Within just two short years, his reputation was formidable. He was said to be a demon incarnate. Not so... because within just two short years he was dead; killed during battle in what is now known as Ocracoke Sound by Lt. Maynard of the British Royal Navy in November of 1718. Unfortunately for Blackbeard, the political climate had changed and the "great or golden age of piracy" would end in less than a decade.

It is said that Blackbeard had fourteen wives, but only took the last one to the altar. What of the remaining thirteen? There is rumor that he murdered each one, in turn, to take the next, but this cannot be substantiated. It is true; however, that he did share at least one of them with members of the crew. I wonder if she would ever be at peace and if her restless spirit might still walk among us. What she would say if she could somehow speak to us — maybe her words would be something like the short reflection that follows.

Ghost of a Wife

When first we met, his dark eyes met mine, and I was held captive. The power of those eyes was unyielding. The danger that lurked behind them beckoned me without mercy. How could I resist? And so we were married, or at least that is what some call it and, we took our pleasure, and he seemed not so stormy. But, alas, he quickly tired of me and in an act of spite and indifference, lent me to the crew. And, indeed, without mercy did he cause my end as surely as if he drew the blade across my throat.

So now he, too, has met the blade, his head severed from his body by Maynard. Maynard hung that horrible head from the bowsprit of the sloop *Jane*. It hung there for months, at first to drip in gore and, later in a briny bath, his braids and fuses matted to the rotting flesh until mid February when they impaled it on a pike in Hampton Yards for all to see and take warning. To this very day there is speculation that his skull was lined in silver and passed from hand to hand, from year to year, and that many have shared drink from it. Some think it is the same skull now at the Mariner's Museum in Newport News, Virginia. Maybe, yes, maybe no — I won't tell. But I will tell you that to this very day, out of the mist, or out of the depths, some can still hear his pleading, "Oh, cock crow", "Oh, cock crow", from the shores of the Island of Ocracoke that is the namesake of that pleading. And I will not tell you if, in truth, as some say, that it is his body that suffers to call out for its severed head for all eternity. But I will tell you with no hint of mercy, that my husband, my Blackbeard, met his just and grisly and inevitable end!

A Visit from Blackbeard

Reflecting upon Blackbeard's life — and death — during the course of my research, a vision of him grew in my mind — "and the smoke it encircled his head like a wreath". So, with my apologies to Clement Clarke Moore I wrote the following adaptation.

'Twas the night before battle and close to the shore
Maynard was planning the pirates' "what's for"
On both sloops the weapons readied with care
Knowing they had no more time to prepare

The sailors were nestled in their hammocks all snug
While each dreamt of slashing some bloodthirsty thug
The watch up on deck and the Captain in his quarters
Had just settled down after a scan of the waters

When three spans away there arose such a clatter
Maynard sprang from his bunk to see what was the matter

A Visit from Blackbeard

He ran straight up on deck and he took up his glass
He stared into the dawn and the mist in the pass

The sunlight was creeping up slow from the sea
And whispered beginnings of the battle to be
When what to his morning blurred eyes next appeared
But the sloop called *Adventure* and the brigand Black-
beard

Teach brandished a sword oh so lively and quick
They all thought it must be a sorcerer's trick
More treacherous than sharks his minions they came
And he whistled and shouted and called them by name

"Now Israel Hands! Now Stede Bonnet too!"
Then he called up of the rest of the twenty-five crew
"Let's give them a broadside" a sloop took the fall
"Now slash away, slash away, slash away all!"

As seabirds before the wild hurricane fly
And screech out a warning in heralding cry
So up in the crosstrees the lookouts did shout
In only light breeze the sloops moved about

"No quarters" cried Maynard; "No quarters" cried Teach
No wind for close haul, and no wind for broad reach
And then in an inkling the blast of the gun
Bursting on deck, there was no place to run

Teach was covered in weapons from his head to his toes
And his raiment dripped fresh with the blood of his foes
A battling midshipman he flung off his back
And looked like a butcher preparing to hack

More fearsome than hellhounds the pirate was seen
With two bandoleers and twelve pistols between
A boot with a dagger and a knife at his waist
He looked like a demon the devil had placed

The length of a cutlass was held tight in his teeth
While the smoke did encircle his head like a wreath
The bellowing blaggards that made up the crew
Had ice in their veins and their weapons drawn too

The sword from his mouth, he took in his hand
And wielded it mightily taking his stand
He made no more sound but went straight to his work
Hacking and slashing in the gore and the murk

He took twenty stab wounds and five from a gun
He broke Maynard's sword, but the pirate was done
On the bowsprit of *Jane* his severed head hung
While his body still twitching o'er the side rail was flung

Then circling the ship six times round stem to stern
Blackbeard's headless body came turn after turn
But all heard it exclaim as the body went down
"Oh, cock crow, oh cock crow", Ocracoke Sound

A Visit from Blackbeard

The Song of the Dying Maid

In the State of Florida, in the Folklife Collection at White Springs, you can find the single paragraph that briefly records the tribal legend upon which this story is based. The ballad "Song of the Dying Maid" currently rewritten by the author, is based, in part, on an earlier version co-authored with Tom Kastle.

The Song of the Dying Maid

At the mouth of the river at the dark of the moon
Each year in the month of May
The Manatee River sings out a tune
As it rolls into the bay
It's a strange crooning sound that began long ago
With the song of a dying maid
On the wind and the water you can hear it still
As twilight starts to fade

Chorus:
And the wind blows
And the river flows
To the sea
And the time goes
As it ebbs and flows
Where is she
Where is she

She was left on board so no tongue could tell
Where they would dig in the night
On a fine silver flute she played so well
In the flickering candlelight
She played on her flute as the ship sank low
Such a mournful and desperate sound
A tale of greed and a tale of woe
And a treasure that's never been found

With a ransom of riches they stole through the night
Those pirates, a bloodthirsty crew
Holding coffers of coin and a prisoner below
A damsel both pure and true
They sailed up the inlet and anchored the ship
Their captive held fast by her chains
She was sealed there inside by the fire's deadly grip
But the story still remains

They sailed silently from the south, threading their way patiently between the mainland and the Keys into Tampa Bay to head east up what is known now as the Manatee River. Their course took them past the places where Cancer and Narvaez and Soto had explored, past the places where the old Spanish watchtowers were deserted and crumbled back into the sand long ago. A day earlier, they came close to the place where Ponce de Leon had explored and attempted to colonize. Futile attempts were made to convert and control the chiefdoms of Tocobaga and Mocoso — cultures whose people had not been seen for over 300 years. The ship glided over the silky rollers under the inky black cover of night at the dark of the moon.

The bloodthirsty lot that was the crew knew well enough what would happen should they be spotted slipping into the bay. They moved under full sail until they started heading closer to land and then dropped all but the jib and stays'l lest they catch the starlight in the larger expanses of canvas. With experienced hands, they were well able to maneuver the small schooner skillfully through the shallows. The lead line revealed the treachery of the sandbars beneath them. Word was passed in short low and rapid whispers to the helm because it was too dark to use hand signals. But no other words were spoken. Jessamine, terrified, had no idea why she had been chained and locked below in her cabin.

The treasure ships of old were part of a golden

fleet that sailed, now, only in memory and legend. It remained the quest of many a man to recover the treasure strewn on the seafloor as the bellies of the great ships were ripped open by storms, reefs, and sand. All that was left was the dream of riches — maybe the chance to find an old piece of parchment with a well-marked trail ending in the elusive X. It could be that some unsuspecting mariner found the map only to have it rifled from his pocket by a shipmate that heard the sailor speak of it during a drunken dream. Or maybe his luck turned when the sailor tried to enlist the help of the wrong sort to explore the trail and wound up in a back alley robbed, unconscious, and betrayed. Finding the trail did not necessarily mean finding the pot of gold at the end.

A small band of pirates who had managed to survive the treachery of their shipmates, manned the schooner. They were skulldugerous scavengers at best, for they had not drawn a single sword or pistol to plunder a merchant ship ripe for the picking, but contented themselves, instead, to wait for others to do the work. Then they would reap the rewards as their own and dispose of all others who might want a share of the booty. These days the loot might be iron stock or finished goods so indispensable to the settlements — or the staple beverage, tea. Maybe it was a cargo of indigo, cotton bales, or tobacco — raw goods that might be taken elsewhere for further processing. The best and easiest to trade and sell (and consume) was the rich, fragrant rum distilled in the islands. But none of it served as the treasure that is the stuff of dreams.

The six were not a band at first. They were, however, each in strong competition to be the most slovenly candidate that had signed articles. But soon they recognized their common malingering traits and malignant thoughts and it drew them to seek each other's company. First in idleness and then in active discourse, they began to fashion their plan. It was, for most of them, the most effort they had ever expended in their inconsequential, lazy lives.

"We all gotta button our lips," warned Beacham, as he eyed the rest of the conspirators with authority and malice. "And forget strong drink 'til after the time comes." A low groan issued from the rest. "I mean it," Beacham's eyes held daggers at the ready. He was born with the power to be a natural leader and so he was until the authorities accused him of being allied with wreckers and purposely running his ship aground so that her cargo could be pilfered. The owners collected the insurance money and, also, he was sure, profited from the actual stolen cargo they had arranged to lose. He was the victim and scapegoat for their illegal commerce. Stripped of his command and his license, embittered and desperate, he fell in with the current unsavory lot.

It was not the plan of the small band to take the ship during some routine score. Sebastian, one of their group, slyly let himself be coerced by the First Mate to turn over an old, but securely cork-ed, barnacle encrusted bottle that held a document snuggly and safely within.

"Give it 'ere," the buckco Mate ordered as he grabbed it. The mate turned it around to light the inside of the bottle as much as possible and could see enough to know that it was important. The Mate immediately declared the confiscated bot-tle and its contents to be property of the crew and brought it to the Captain.

When last on shore, Sebastian had found the relic lodged in some rocks along the shore where the tide had forced it at some point in the distant past. He could not read so he took it to Beacham along with the three pieces of eight that had been rolled tightly inside what looked to be the genuine article, a treasure map! *Why would someone put a treasure map in a bottle? It doesn't make any sense.* He spent no further time thinking about it. In any event, if the map were real, there was no use in trying to find and recover the goods on their own.

"Let's let 'em do it for us," slippery Sebastian sported a wide toothy grin that showed spaces here and there.

Pit perked up and mumbled in mush mouth, "Den wekin waze 'em." His eye squint eye glowed with greed, "Donneed res o' dem anywaze."

They all stared at the map. The paper was un-expectedly crisp with all of the script, diagrams, directions, and coordinates clear and perfect. The cork had been sealed into the bottle with wax to prevent any leakage and the parchment rolled tightly and tied with a bit of thin line to keep out the rays of the sun. As an additional protection against the rocks and waves, close-woven netting, now almost worn away and mingled in bits with the barnacles, had served its purpose well. Beacham purloined a piece of mending canvas and copied the map. While he did so, he tried to remember, as best he could, where the minutes and seconds would land them. He would know where they were heading and, better still, it would help him be able to plot the course away from where they would leave the bodies of those not among the six.

Even though the original crew members were despicable pirates, they received welcome at any port in the islands where a dockmaster, for a small "inspection fee", would easily let them unload their cargo and peruse a fake manifest with blind eye and no questions. Unscrupulous traders would buy up the goods right at the dock and load it back on legitimate carriers, perhaps and on its way to the originally intended recipients who had now paid for it twice. Sometimes, the Captain mused at the possibility that some of the cotton bales just circulated in unending transit. But this time, when they fitted the ship, it would be for a prize most rare. He, too, shared the same dream of greed with every other hunter of unearned wealth. The officer had no illusions about his livelihood and certainly none about the tenuous loyalty of his crew. Sometimes it was necessary to turn a member or two over to the authorities if the powers that be were in need of appeasement. This happened only when some self-righteous petty politician or member of the peerage wanted to gain favor with the public or with superiors. *No matter,* he thought to himself, *Just part of the cost of doing business.* He DID mind, when on occasion, the "inspection fee" was raised to fill the purse of one of those same politicians and nobles. *And they label me as a thief!* It caused him to break a wry smiled and snort.

At one of the islands, a young woman asked permission to come aboard the schooner and requested the Captain to take her on as a passenger. Her story was the essence of tender age and innocence but as old as time. Her father, for his own profit, wanted her to marry a disgusting and offensive old man.

"Chattel!" she spoke bitterly, her hazel eyes brimming with tears perched to fall, "That's all I am to my father. And he knows that my heart belongs to my darling Jimmy who will return from sea within the month. Oh, please take me to your next port of call where I can arrange to meet my Jimmy." So, on a whim, Captain Weston accepted the fee for her passage and assigned her private accommodations in the small cabin that was ordinarily occupied by the First Mate and Bo'sun. They were not pleased and made uncouth and unsavory remarks about what they might do if they were assigned to the same cabin with her.

Her small, hastily packed bag was thrown unceremoniously into the cabin by a boy of about her same age, probably fifteen or so. She sat for a long time clutching the bag, the tears now falling fully down her face. Her resolve was strong, but it was no match for her trepidation in pursuing such a bold and frightening action. She shivered in fear and loneliness, but it was too late to change her mind. The ship had slipped the mooring lines and was making rapid progress on the evening tide and a favorable wind.

Almost at sunset, the boy returned with a mug of water and bowl of stew that was heavily seasoned with datil peppers from Minorca and set to grow up north in the La Florida. It was far too spicy for her taste, but she ate it anyway. The burning on her tongue surpassed the burning of her tears which was a good thing. Afterwards, she laid the dishes aside and pulled out a long thin bag fastened at the top with a draw string and removed the contents, a shiny silver flute. It had been a gift from her mother on Jessamine's eighth birthday. The girl listened, enraptured by the sound as her mother played her own flute to lull the sun to sleep and welcome it in the morning. Note by note, melody by melody, year by year, the girl learned to weave the songs of mirth and mournfulness. She and her mother would play together in glorious harmonies. And when her mother died, Jessamine would lay the notes upon the air in hopes that not even the grave could silence the songs that they shared. It was only then that she finally understood that it was the ability of her mother's music to fill the empty places that so captivated her as a child. It was for this reason, in this small space, at this time that the girl played a mournful song in tempo with the movement of the ship. It allowed her to travel in tandem with the roll of the waves and not suffer from their unfamiliar constant motion. It allowed her to focus on her longing for Jimmy.

The ship sailed for three days and for three nights, and on the morning of the fourth day the lookout hollered, "Land, Ho!" from the crosstrees. And there it was, barely visible in the low clouds and morning mist — the island. The crew gave up a cheer and danced a jig. They almost salivated with anticipation of the wealth that awaited them. They came as close to the island as they dared and dropped anchor. The map did not show any information about the surrounding waters and the Captain was seasoned enough not to come any closer even though the sunlight revealed the clear and inviting shades of blue and green in the water beneath them. It was too easy to be fooled about the depth and size of each individual mound of coral. The Captain was lowered in his own small gig with three others to serve as a landing party. They were well armed and each took a bag of water, a measure of cheese, and some jerky as well as a tinder box and a length of strong rope. Captain Weston carried the map in his inside vest pocket with a small compass. They each took an oar, rowed to shore, beached the boat, dragged it up the sand, and slogged it through the mangroves to where they found more solid ground. There, they made it fast on the sizable stump of a twisted tree with smooth bark. Weston withdrew the map from his pocket, checked his compass, and led them forward into the bush.

Jessamine was elated! Finally, they were at the next port! Soon they would let her out of the cabin where they had kept her with care and she would be able to arrange to meet Jimmy. She put her few belongings in her small bag and waited and dreamed of her darling. But no one came. *What was to become of her?*

There did not appear to be much on the island except a few tall palms, pines, and underbrush clinging to the sand that was held there by the protective and pervasive mangroves along the water's edge. Here and there, worn lumps of weathered coral were visible. As they moved inland, they would change direction according to the officer's command. The ground was much more substantial as they neared the place marked by the X. Suddenly one member of the party pulled aside a bush and fell unexpectedly into a deep cave of coral. The remainder of the group heard him groaning a distance downwards from where they all stood fast, not wanting to suffer the same fate.

"Are ye all right?" the Captain yelled down into the hole.

"I tink I broke me leg," the crewman wailed. The three at the top made their lengths of different size cordage together with a series of sheet bends. As luck would have it, another tree stump was located a convenient distance from the cave entrance. It was not purely a straight drop, so Weston and one of the hands descended slowly and carefully — the coral here had not been exposed so completely to the elements and could cut a hand and even a carelessly maneuvered line. Finally, they arrived at the bottom of the pit where they found their shipmate. He had stopped groaning. His misshapen leg folded behind him and the many cuts to his face made by the coral, it turned out, were the least of his problems. More so were the small streamlined shapes that undulated slowly about the edges of the cave. Even in the low light, their golden bodies were visible. The treasure, if it were there, remained guarded by a battalion of slithering sentries. Both men drew their swords and began swiftly and deftly to slice off the heads of the reptilian protectors. Deadly snakes seemed to appear from every crack and crevasse. In a frenzy of fear and adrenaline, the men vanquished the guardians. In great numbers the vipers now writhed, headless, in the throes of death.

The men turned quickly in all directions still poised to fight. But it was over. Still, they moved slowly and carefully down a passage that opened at the north side of the cave keeping hands and heads well away from the walls. The map had no more secrets to offer and was placed back in the waiting vest pocket. For a while there were places where the cave allowed sunlight to filter down inside, but soon only darkness lay before them. It was impossible to continue. They retraced their steps and worked their way back up the line to the top and breathed heavily of the fresh salt air.

"Where's Giblet?" the topman queried.

"Vipers," the Captain couldn't quash the shiver that ran the length of his spine.

The third man experienced the same silent recollection, "Think we got 'em all, but there's no way to know." The men ate their small meal on foot moving much more slowly and carefully than they had on the way in.

Blindfolded, prodded, and pulled, Jessamine walked stiffly up the companionway to a fate she dared not imagine. It was more than stiffness, she was petrified with fear. But, to her surprise, she was allowed to walk around within a small cordoned area. She guided herself around the small square by following the path of the rope with her hands; they did not remove the blindfold. It was good, she thought, to be able to breathe freely of the warm breeze. The crew hustled her below when the shore party returned. The small bowl of stew the boy brought to her that evening seemed less savory with age, but there was also a small piece of hard bread and, of course, water. Food, even if it was old, was not wasted aboard ship. Again, she played her flute for company and comfort. She imagined that she and her mother were playing a duet. Her sadness was reflected in the sorrowful notes she played

The next day slings of supplies were prepared and carried to the cave by a shore party of ten. They took torches, oil, candles, rope, shovels, sacks, along with basic rations and fresh water. Each of them carried a long sword. Beachum and Sebastian were among them. The two didn't really want to work, but the thought of being among the first to see the glittering treasure was too tempting. Beachum was no coward, but vipers were a formidable enemy. Sebastian, on the other hand, was almost as slippery as the snakes and his personal motto was, "Better you than me!" Beachum knew this and watched his co-conspirator carefully at all times. And the First Mate watched every one of the nine in his command with a non-blinking eye every second. No one could be trusted. Not when they could almost smell the gold.

There were branches jutting off the main tunnel. In pairs, they explored each possibility leaving a trail of shells on the way in and collecting them on the way out except a few to mark the places already investigated. They worked round the clock. It was slow progress. Energy and enthusiasm began to fade. The party of ten traded places with ten of their shipmates and the searching continued, uninterrupted. This occurred daily for three days. At least they had finished the putrid old stew and were eating fresh broth filled with large chunks of fish and seasoned with seaweed. Unfortunately, the men found several more of the fanged fiends as they combed the tunnels. At least the next two victims of the deadly venom met their demise with full and happy stomachs.

Their passenger-cum-prisoner was allowed, now, to take her meals on deck inside her little square of existence. Although she could not see what she was eating, she was as grateful as everyone, for the lovely change of menu. Even with the daily tasks of shipboard life, several of the crew, particularly the slovenly band, began to fixate on the beauty of the young maiden. The Captain had warned them that, as a member of a prominent family, she would serve a much better hostage alive and unharmed. And she would certainly fetch a much higher price on the slave market if she remained untouched.

Sebastian felt himself stiffen in response to the thought of unwrapping the long golden braid that reached down to the small of her back. Pit imagined following a course below the braid. Not even Beachum was immune to the adventures that his mind contrived, even as he focused on the plan. The other three in their group were ashore when Pit grew close enough to smell the overpowering invitation of her femininity. He didn't have the brain, willpower, or presence of mind to think about the consequences of his actions. He stepped under the rope and grabbed her. She shrieked in surprise, not able to see her assailant, she continued screaming.

Unfortunately for Pit, the Captain was close enough to grab an unused belaying pin from the rail and blast the worthless worm across the side of his head. The injured man fell to the deck clasping the blindfold. Jessamine could now see the Captain, the onboard crew, and the whole ship quite clearly. There was no chance of using her as a hostage anymore. She could identify all those who stood on deck. Not having any clue about the gravity of what had just happened, she profusely thanked the Captain. Having gained her trust, Weston saw no reason to blindfold her or confine her in any way. That evening she played a merry tune on her flute to help the sun to sleep. "I can see now how sometimes good comes out of evil," she said out loud to the walls of the cabin, naively thinking to restore some of her faith in mankind, and clinging to the hope that she would survive this ordeal and see here true Love when it was over.

On the morning of the fourth day both the Captain and Beachum were with the group on shore. The two of them decided to explore the surrounding area in an attempt to find easier access to the cave. They found no other entrance, but they did find an overhang covered at the front with tattered remains of old sailcloth. Inside the small shelter, Beachum finally found the answer to his question as to why someone would put a map in a bottle. The remains that lay on the makeshift cot sported threadbare clothing but no skin between it and the dried pitted bones. Small creatures had long since eaten their fill of the soft tissue. A bottle, similar in shape and design to the one that had held the map was positioned in what had once been a living hand. Inside a small leather pouch they found parchment, quill, and ink. Here was the man who sent the message. In desperation, with a very slim chance of success, it was the only means he had at his disposal to effect his rescue. And it worked to a degree, but certainly not on a timely basis! The reason he had been marooned would be a mystery for the ages.

They left the corpse in his self-made tomb and began a search of one of the passage ways and found what others might have considered a dead end. But Beachum noticed that the apparently fallen bits of coral were not quite haphazardly placed. Weston looked up at the ceiling of the passage and all along the walls and saw that there was no indication of a natural landside or contributing erosion. They had found it! The Captain moved to one side and inserted his torch into a small space while Beachum stood with his sword at the ready. Three vipers hurtled their slinky bodies out of the pile. They were headless and hapless in short order. The process was repeated several times at different locations in the mound of stones. The two warily deconstructed the doorway to what they were sure was the entrance to the long-closed vault. When the last rock was relocated, they lighted another torch and pushed it inside the rounded opening lest any skulking sentry still survived. They stomped on the ground outside the door seeking to wake and flush out any living thing that might lurk inside. But all was silence. Almost timidly, they took a peek. Their eyes drank in the color of riches as the torchlight flickered upon it — a profusion of precious metals gold and silver — a bouquet of gems red and blue and green — the roundness of pearls white and black — coinage galore. They were awestruck. They were overcome by the beauty. They were thrilled with their success. And they were infused with avarice. One thought dominated all others in each of their minds, "*MINE.*"

It took another three days to transport and secure the portion of the treasure they had deposited in the cargo hold. The Captain explained the wisdom of leaving the remainder for their next voyage. The rocks and stones at the front of the treasure trove were replaced, this time giving the illusion of a natural occurrence. Weston took care to note the correct path, using his own code on the reverse side of the map and placed it, once again, inside his vest pocket. Beachum did much the same. And so they set a course back north to divide some of the spoils and bury the rest. This time, the map to mark the treasure site would be torn in random pieces and divided among them. Each evening, on their return voyage, they were calmed by the different lullabies that Jessemine played for the sinking sun and those not on the dogwatch were wakened each morning as she played to greet the new day. In appreciation of her service to the crew, the Captain gave the maiden with the long golden braid a silver necklace that held a single, tiny emerald that enhanced the green in her eyes. She was learning to love the sea and began to understand what had drawn her Jimmy to it. She never forgot that it was he whom she loved.

The schooner moved upriver in the darkness and put into a small inlet where they made fast to the mangroves. To insure her compliance in staying onboard, despite any of her pleadings, Captain Weston ordered her chained by the ankles to the foot of her bunk where she waited in sorrow and disbelief. She had come to regard him much more kindly than she did her own father. *How could he be so cruel?* Her mind wallowed in betrayal and self pity as she sobbed. She was truly alone; no other was left aboard. The eerie silence of the abandonment fell upon her. She imagined that the cabin was shrinking in size as the walls closed in. She drew halting hard breaths. It struck her for the first time that she was going to die. How foolish she had been to come willingly to her doom. There were no more tears, just the anticipation of the end.

Being pirates one and all, not a single member of the crew was content to be left behind when the treasure was buried. None wanted to be shorted in their current share. It would have been impossible for each of them to take their full share without risking exposure. Plus there would have been no way for any single man to carry such a load. So they decided to meet later at a prearranged time and place, reconstruct the map, and come back for the remainder of the loot. Each wanted to mark the location of the site in their minds, but the map would serve as insurance lest they forget important details. They worked together to carry the considerable burden which they had sewn in heavy canvas bags and locked in a number of wooden chests. To a man, they grasped their immediate divvy and, when the map was drawn and torn, placed their piece of the puzzle secretly on their person. It was done, finally. The dream was theirs!

Jessemine needed now, more than ever, to play her flute. She struggled to reach it behind her on the other side of the small table for she was unable to stand with her ankles made fast by the manacles. She stretched as far as she could and was fortunate to lay a single finger tip upon her mother's gift. With great difficulty she inched the instrument closer and was finally able to grasp it. But in this effort, she overturned the oil lamp that was also on the table. The liquid spilled across the surface and onto the floor, and with it the flame. The song she played was not for the sun. It was her own song, her final song — the last greeting to welcome death and the last lullaby for her final sleep.

Each man was lost in his own dream as he headed back down the dark path to the ship. They each heard the sweet, sorrowful, sound of a flute and came to know the meaning of the music as each dream turned to a nightmare. The slovenly crew slit each throat from behind and gathered the bits of the map. They could hear the flute from below as they boarded the ship, but had not yet grasped its meaning. In their haste and greed they loosed the lines and headed from the intlet toward the mouth of the river. The song of the flute gave way to the groaning, moaning melody emanating from the river itself. It was such a terrifying sound that these hardened and heartless cowards trembled in fear. It was then that the flames shot through the deck and up the rig to the sails and all was lost to the dark of the moon and the trick of the tide.

It is said in local native legend, that if you open your mind and your ears in the month of May at the dark of the moon when the tide is just right, you can still hear the song of the dying maid. It is remembered and repeated by the river in the place where she played her the last note on the silver flute that her mother had given her when she was just a child. And it is wise not to contemplate the melody lest you understand it all too well.

Alien Monsters of the Great Lakes

Long, long ago there were huge rivers of ice that flowed across the land and scoured and scarred it — mercilessly moving rocks and stones and boulders — gouging and carving — changing the earth forever. In time, they melted away and became rivers and streams branching out to the east and to the west and to the south. They melted into small lakes and into five very, very big lakes now know as the Great Lakes.

For a long time the world inside those Great Lakes flourished with plants and creatures of all sizes and descriptions. There were trout and whitefish. There were sturgeons and sticklebacks. There were crayfish and clams. There were gulls and herons. There were otters and beavers and there were even teeny-tiny, teensy-weensy microscopic critters called plankton. Some of the plankton were plants and some of the plankton were animals. Imagine that! Plants and animals swimming and floating all around the lakes, so many of them that one couldn't see but a few feet down into the water — and, after a while, there were people, too.

For a long time the trout and the sturgeon and the sticklebacks and the crayfish and clams and the herons and the gulls and the otters and the beavers and the plankton and even the people lived together in relative harmony. The plant plankton used the sun to grow and make oxygen and there was just enough of everything for everyone. Of course, it could not be said that everyone got along with everybody all the time — after all, the animal plankton and the clams ate the plant plankton and sometimes the animal plankton would eat each other. The sticklebacks and crayfish and the otters and beavers and heron and gulls ate any fish that they could catch. And the people would eat the fish and other animals from the lakes and from the land and use the skins to make clothing and shelter and utensils and even musical instruments, but everyone had a special place they called home, and nobody traveled too far from there most of the time.

After a while, people started making canoes and rafts and traveling further, and they brought animals and plants with them — sometimes because they wanted to, and sometimes without knowing it! People began traveling down the rivers, across the lakes and across the oceans in large double-hulled canoes and sailing ships with many masts and large cargo ships powered by steam and then by oil. Many, many people started moving all around the world and all around the Great Lakes.

The more people, the more they would bring with them — just a few plants and animals that they needed. The more people, the more they would take — from the Lakes — just a few plants and animals that they needed. With so many people bringing and taking and thinking it was only what was needed, nobody noticed it when the aliens came. Nobody paid any attention as they hid in ballast tanks and fastened themselves secretly to the bottom of ships and swam silently up the seaway and were discarded into the sewers or pretended to be dead bait and were thrown into the depths.

There were signs, there were portents, but most of the people just thought that the Lakes were so vast that they would take care of themselves. Besides, at first, there were only a few fish that bore the marks, where the lamprey had drained the blood leaving the fish dead or close to death. Only old people remember, these days, about the piles of rotting, stinking, alewives on the beaches. Never mind that those zebra mussels can be pretty annoying when they block water intake pipes. Besides the Lakes are in fine shape, look at how clear the water is!

Those invaders can be sneaky and deceptive, and they're here even as this story is being written. Though seemingly small, they are monsters of great proportion, because they are exactly like everyone else who thinks that they are bringing and taking only what they need. Zebra mussels are only eating the plankton that they need, but as their numbers grow, they will need more and more. They are voracious.

For a long time the sturgeons and the sticklebacks and the crayfish and the clams and herons and gulls and the otters and the beavers and the plankton and even the people lived together in relative harmony. The plant plankton used the sun to grow and make oxygen and there was just enough of everything for everyone. The animal plankton and the clams ate the plant plankton and sometimes the animal plankton ate each other. The sticklebacks and crayfish ate the plankton and the heron and the gulls and the otters and the beavers ate any fish that they could catch, and the people ate the fish and they would all breathe the same oxygen.

How clear the water is in Lake Michigan these days — one can see down a long, long way, further than ever before. Look down into the harbors. Look down into the deeper water away from shore on a calm day where sunlight now travels all the way to the bottom to reveal what is below. How clear the water is. No fear of monsters here! Still — where is the plant plankton that used to conceal the depths and make the oxygen? What will the sturgeon and trout and sticklebacks and crayfish and herons and gulls and otters and beavers, and humans eat?

And...

How — will they all breathe?

Well Met

The storm blew them helplessly off course. Lightning split the sky. The thunder repeated a continuous broadside. Winds whipped the waves into a frothy, frenzy that flung the ship in fury from crest to trough. And they were taken down.

Sunlight poured over the horizon casting light upon the bodies tossed haphazardly along the sandy shore. Bodies cycled in seemingly endless watery motion over and over with each rolling wave. Bits and pieces of the once proud merchant ship joined the tumult at the shore. Most of the twenty-six crew as well as the cargo shifted far out to sea and now rested on the bottom with Davey Jones.

As the day matured, a few of the seemingly lifeless victims stirred and awoke to find themselves stranded — where?

Jacko examined a long gash on his left shin sealed by dried blood and salt. The same salt that burned his bleary eyes as the sun seared every part of his mostly exposed skin; the pounding of the surf and the reef had ripped most of his clothes away.

Along the strand, he saw that those now stirring found themselves in similar distress. Some were scraped severely by the coral. Some were marked by the stings of jellyfish, and one or two were missing a limb that had been ripped from them by the impact of the ship as it hit the reef and the heavy rigging fell. Not many survived. The few that did slowly came together stopping to shake those who remained in stillness and silence hoping to find more of the ship's company alive. They checked for any sign of life with only occasional success.

So here they were, only thirteen of the once proud crew. Without uttering a word, those with any strength moved those who had none, under the shade of a stand of coconut palms. In a daze, the men retrieved the few lifeless bodies of the ship's company that made it to shore and laid those six also in the shade. They were Simmons the sailmaker, the surly boatswain, Tuttle, with his ample beard; the two old veterans Tommy and James; and a couple of indistinguishable greenhorns whose names no one could recall, side by side just as they had once served.

Overcome with hunger, thirst, fatigue, and pain from their own injuries, they sat, stunned and flanked on either side by the dead and the dying, and each, in turn, shed the tears of anguish and loss and grief and fear. Their immediate need for food and water left little time to think about rest — or pain. Good fortune had not abandoned them completely. Several of the heavy fruit had fallen from the tree and lay on the sand, for not one of them men had the strength to shinny up a trunk to reach them at the top. Also, four of the men had the great good luck not to lose their britches, but more importantly, they did not lose the rope belts that held them up. This was because the belts also held their rigging knives and marlinspikes. They pierced a couple of the brown hairy husks to drink and share the refreshing liquid. Grizzled old Greeby gathered the sharp serrated homes of long-dead mollusks and they scraped out the sweet, white meat of the coconuts and thanked the heavens for the meager meal.

Six of the hardiest survivors formed two groups. Jacko took Greeby and young Jim, the whistle player. Andrew, the only officer left hail and hardy, took Patel who had joined the ship's company in Chennai, and a seasoned but dull fellow they called Bunn. The search parties walked in opposite directions under the shade of the palms to each end of the stand and then headed inland through the large ferns and bushes of fragrant blooms. Each group took with them the crude bowls and hoped to return with water. Realizing that they might need weapons, they each chose a long, sturdy stick that they collected a short distance away from the beach and, taking turns with the blades, sharpened an end as a ready spear should they find game.

Two able seamen remained at the makeshift camp. McGinty had once carried a hod and practiced a bit of masonry before a brush with the law caused the circumstance of him winding up at sea. It turned out that he found it was far preferable to his lot on land. Somehow shipboard discipline agreed with him, as did the fact of strong drink being inaccessible most of the time. Beanpole, also there, a whiny but wiry hand, executed orders with the speed of a snail stuck in molasses. They combed the beach to gather the wooden bits of wreckage that had washed ashore to use as firewood. They also hoped to find some larger pieces of the ship or maybe small useful items that were light enough to be carried by the waves and not strewn somewhere at the bottom of the sea. As luck would have it, they found only a few wooden spoons. The tide carried large sections of canvas ripped from the full sails that trailed various lengths of line from the running rigging. They held out hope for a barrel of salted meat or maybe a cask of rum, but such luck was not to be had. Still, good finds, these items were added to the sailmaker's ditty bag that held needles, several lengths of whipping thread, some marline, and a sailor's palm.

Of no help except to keep a semblance of lookout, were the wounded. Josiah, a former slave whose skin gleamed like polished ebony, now nursed a broken ankle. As a fugitive, he could still be returned to his master. But he had managed to earn and save enough money from his share of cargo revenue to buy his own freedom. He was his own man. The gunner, formally a strapping solid block of a man with a fiery red beard and loud rasping voice, now lacked the presence of mind to feed himself or form a simple sentence due to a severe head wound. Lars lay unconscious as his life ebbed from the place where his right arm had been taken just below the shoulder by a bit of the falling rig; the rope tourniquet stemmed but could not stop the flow. A Maori with signs of nobility carved and colored into his face as was the custom of his people, lingered stubbornly to life, breathing in what was surely a death rattle. A shark had feasted upon on a large ragged mouthful from the sailor's left side. The native had been quite an artist in his time and used India ink and needle to transform the odd bit of ivory or bone into a masterpiece of story. Stumpy, the ship's cook, would never again be able to use his single remaining leg.

On the path, the small but scrappy wild boar that ran a zigzag path through the thicket was an unwilling and wily bit of prey. The men struggled to surround it. The creature flailed its tiny tusks just missing the calves of its predators but met its end as Jacko plunged the wooden spear with great speed and force into the porcine eye. The fluid and blood poured from the now empty socket. The creature shook violently and fell silent at Jacko's feet that now rested in the pool of gore. Jacko felt pleasure in this act—more than that it gave him a sense of power. He had, he remembered, this same feeling as a youth, when he successfully caught a wild rabbit in a make-shift trap, hung the squirming furry thing from a tree limb, and ripped the skin from it while it still twitched with life. He hadn't known before then that rabbits could scream, but the sound made him aware, for the first time, of his manhood. The scream-like squeal of the pig in its final breath, again, brought him to a state of ecstasy.

Young Jim who had no stomach for it, turned away and fought hard to retain the contents of his stomach. Greeby removed the weapon and bound the animal to it with vines. He and Jim, now recovered from what he hoped would be his last hunt, each put an end of the spear on a shoulder and shared the load as they walked and continued to search for water. Jacko shook himself back to present time and joined them. They still needed water. The shadows were getting longer and they knew it would not be much time before they would be forced to return to camp. At least they were not empty handed. Greeby and Jim became uneasy as they seemed to hear the wind move the leaves to whisper in the evening breeze.

Andrew and his companions headed into the wind and followed a small breeze that carried the sweet smell of fresh water. They quickened their steps at the sound of a small stream and rushed to it. All three greedily cupped both hands and drank to quench their mighty thirst. After a very short rest, they continued upstream for a while but they, too, could see the shadows stretching long and lean. They filled the bowls and made their way back toward camp. As the sunlight began to depart, they all became silent and moved in great haste. Patel tried not to think of the many legends he remembered from his childhood about the spirits and creatures of the night. It seemed as if they heard a voice whispering to them each time from a different direction. Sometimes it encircled them. It was a voice that spoke without words.

The sun measured only two fingers from the horizon when the search parties returned. They sliced the pig in thin strips and cooked it over a low fire so as to conserve wood. They divided the water. Jacko gnawed with relish at the tiny bits of meat that were left on the skull, some only partially cooked including the single remaining eye. No one challenged him, for it was not to their taste. Most of them made it a point to steer clear of the likes of Jacko. As each batch of meat was done, a strip was given, in turn, to every man. This did not take very long because the two most gravely wounded no longer had any need of food. They laid Lars and the Maori alongside the others who could not be saved. They must find a place to bury the now decaying bodies of the dead. Not much conversation passed between those who were still living. Better to rest and talk tomorrow. It was full dark now and the meat was all cooked.

Perhaps it was because they were so fatigued or perhaps they didn't have the energy or because they were still in shock, no one thought to post a watch. In deep slumber they did not hear it come in the night. They rested unaware — until the first light of day. It was Andrew who arose before the others. For a short time he wished that he was still asleep and all of this was a bad dream. He hadn't noticed yet, and when he did, he broke a cold sweat and knew that it was not a bad dream but a living nightmare. As he scanned the neatly placed bodies of his fallen comrades, he could see an empty space at the top of each and every neck — not a single head remained on the bloody stumps that oozed above each set of shoulders. The macabre nature of the scene was intensified by the communion of small sand crabs that were holding a banquet as they covered the wounds. Andrew was too weak to stand. Involuntarily, he twisted his body to the side and vomited. When he recovered, he roused the able crew who, when they saw the decapitated bodies, all reacted similarly to Andrew — all except Jacko. They each took some water but were not able to face any kind of food.

It was imperative that they bury the bodies RIGHT AWAY. They had no boat and could not bury them at sea. Andrew remembered that they had passed a deep gulley a fair distance from the camp. Temporary stretchers were constructed of canvas and sticks each capable of carrying two bodies at once. They had originally laid seven dead crew members beside each other—now there were nine. It would take two trips. Two able seamen would stay behind to guard the camp and begin to build more protective quarters. Each man was now armed, including the injured. Those at camp swapped shifts at gathering materials and building. Rocks and large shell bits were dug out with coconut shell shovels and placed in a square of canvas to be hauled back to the site. A primitive floor plan large enough to allow for a small storage space and room enough for the eleven to lie side by side was outlined by shells. McGinty knew how to burn the shells to get lime and mix it with sand and water to make tabby. The mixture would hold the shells and rocks together to form the walls.

Along the path and at the site, the burial detail was complicated by the insects that buzzed around the desiccated corpses. The inimical creatures drawn to the blood had no preference for dead or living flesh. The men were plagued with stings and bites. One by one, they laid the fallen to rest in the gulley. They pushed as much loose soil as they could into the hole and cut palm fronds which they built in several layers on top of the soil. It was not, perhaps, the best of graves, but it was what they could do. The task took most of the morning. Andrew, the only surviving officer among the crew, spoke words of comfort and farewell to the departed and then led the six to the stream to gather water before returning to camp. This time they explored further upstream and could see evidence of an old lava flow as the terrain sloped upwards. By the time they filed the canvas bags that they had sewn the night before, the shadows, once again, appeared across the landscape. And, once again, they fell silent and shivered to the taunting of the wordless whispers.

Together at camp, the group, now numbering three wounded and eight able, shared what was left of the pork, supplemented their meal with coconut bits, and drank freely of the water. Several of them nursed and scratched their many bites. They also admired and appreciated the foundation for the small structure that was dug in at about one foot in depth and rose just more than a foot above the ground; a beginning. It was at least some small boundary between them and whatever was out there, perhaps symbolic at this point but necessary to their sanity. Tomorrow they would all work to complete it.

The events of the previous night and the worrying whispers heard along the path near dusk were now common knowledge. It made them fearful. Andrew suggested that the whispers might just be the result of an evening breeze that played an unusual song in the leaves as night fell. As the person of rank, it was his duty to quell the growing anxiety of the men — and the anxiety that he, himself, felt. But there was no way to explain away the missing heads or the indelible picture of the gaping wounds at the end of each neck that could have been made by the jagged teeth of a very large creature. The scene etched itself eternally in each of their minds. Jacko drank in every gory detail as it was recounted, incredulously, again and again by those who could find it possible to speak of the horror and make observations. Despite the growing unrest and disorder, they could all agree that they were NOT alone.

Andrew bade them to run through the possibilities and strategies over and over until they could no longer stay awake. The whistle player who had, somehow, managed to hold on to his instrument as he clung to a bit of wreckage, now played a soothing melody as he and Bunn were left on guard duty. They had several weapons at the ready including spears and large, sharp lava rocks. Night sounds hummed and tweeted and shrieked around them, sounds that they were not awake to hear the night before and — something else — an underlying whisper. One that they recognized only too well and it made their blood run cold. But they heard no sound of approach by any creature large or small. Bunn walked a short distance in the direction of the water (not having any inclination to head into the bush) and relieved himself, but as he did so, he faced the vast ocean and heard nothing but the sound of the waves as they rolled in and were sucked back. He peered up at the stars trying to find one that was familiar. Surely, only a short time had passed when he turned to walk back. But when he got there, he did not see his shipmate. He strained his eyes to search up and down the beach in the dim light of the stars; his companion would not have gone into the jungle anymore than, he, himself. Where was Jim? He hesitated to wake the others because he would have to explain why he let the other guard out of his site. He counted the sleepers, nine. All accounted for. He called for his musical friend in a low voice but there was no reply. He had to wake the rest.

In startled awareness they all jumped to their feet and there was great confusion as they each grabbed a weapon; some leapt and stood at attention where they were. A couple of men were outside the small barrier. Jacko's eyes glinted and his nostrils flared at the smell of blood. The men all stood at the ready. But it was already too late. Stumpy clenched a spear from his seated position supporting himself gently against the foundation. Josiah, too weak to walk, stood while putting most of his weight upon a spear. The gunner was propped against the foundation, oblivious and drooling from the right side of his mouth. The able bodied each held a spear in one hand and a large rock in the other. But there was one who remained prone upon the ground in the center of the space, one who was bereft of his head, one whose blood still pumped from the severed arteries in his ravaged neck. When the realization came to each of them, now, only ten still breathing, it was as if they were made of stone. They did not move—for a long time. They kept their watch in this way until the first rays of sunlight made lines of red outward from the horizon on the grayness of the water.

The sunshine brought only total exhaustion as

the adrenaline dissipated. Even the brightness of day could not lessen the dread that overwhelmed their minds. Andrew did his best to assign building tasks to occupy the beleaguered crew. Their frantic state of mind was almost palpable. There was no shortage of work because they needed to continue building the shelter. McGinty still supervised construction. The only one who seemed not to suffer any loss of energy was Jacko who volunteered to take the latest victim to the burial spot by himself. Andrew knew it unwise to let anyone go unaccompanied and joined Jacko. When he picked up the poles. His muscles rebelled and ached as they trudged along. Because he was at the rear, it was impossible not to view the grisly, mutilated corpse as the insects gathered to engorge themselves on the remains of the unfortunate victim. Andrew thought about the young sailor, Jim. He was perhaps one of the youngest among the crew out for his first voyage. He remembered the joyfulness of the jigs that the fellow played upon his penny whistle up at the forebits. He also reflected upon the mournfulness of the slow airs that wafted on the wind and filled each heart with the longing for home. Andrew wished that he could recall the melody of just one tune to hum as they laid the lad with the others. But his mind could not find the notes, so, instead, he murmured a scant few words.

Andrew suggested that they might explore a bit further up the stream because it was still only a few hours after sunrise. Perhaps they would be able to get a better view of their surroundings if they climbed up the gentle slope of the volcano. Jacko agreed amiably. This did not remedy the officer's unfavorable gut reaction that grew each time he looked into the emptiness of Jacko's eyes. Against the possibility that they might be able to start mapping the island at some point, Andrew brought the India ink, the writing twig, and a small square of canvas to record the lay of the land. They had enough water and could get more when they needed. It was not an easy trek. Even though the lava had been ground down by countless years of wearing weather, it was still rough and cracked. One of those cracks could easily capture and injure an ankle. The sun was a bit past its zenith when they reached the top. As they progressed upward, the rock had not yet crumbled to a texture hospitable enough for any tiny seed to take root. Poised at the edge of the caldera, both men stared into the abyss of what appeared to be a long inactive rift. It showed no escaping acrid steam, made no semblance of sound, displayed no tremor, and had no flicker of molten rock below.

Jacko's eyes glinted when he thought about how long he might be able to hear the outcries of the officer beside him before the flailing form sank into the suffocating ash and splattered on the hard surface below. He could envision the rent flesh and the crushed and flattened skull. So deep was he in his fantasy that he did not notice that he was listing on an angle that would surely send his own body careening over the edge. Andrew grabbed the back of the rope belt that was wrapped around Jacko's waist and drew him back to safety using the last ounce of strength that he could muster. Jolted out of his revere, Jacko abandoned his fantasy for the time being.

From their vantage point they were able to see the large stand of palm trees that marked their encampment on the east side of the sole spec of an island. The vastness of the empty ocean surrounded it as far as the eye could see. The camp was the only area that showed a sandy surface. Lava seemed to have flowed in the remaining three directions all the way to the sea. It was a largely inhospitable coastline and a major miracle that the ship had chanced to impact in a way for the men to have access to the sand and not the treacherous, deadly lava. With the sun now at a slight angle, they could also see the coral reef that surrounded the land mass. How any living creature made its way here they could not surmise and considered themselves most fortunate to have found the pig and hoped that there were many more. They did see a few large birds soaring above them and heard some birdsong when they walked the jungle path.

Andrew pursued his favorite occupation. He dipped the writing stick into the ink and drew the shape of the island, noting its features, and a simple arrow showing north. He and Jacko estimated the island to be about two miles in diameter, a nearly perfect circle. They had some water while the ink dried and then headed back down the slope. On their way back, they took the familiar path along the stream and picked up the stretcher they left at the hollow. Andrew hastened his pace when they heard the all too familiar whispering. This time it spoke with a discernible malevolence. Jacko found in that tone a kindred spirit and began to grow curious about its nature.

The two returned to camp to see that McGinty and the others had completed the first of what they hoped would be several sturdy structures. The solid walls rose a full six feet above the sand! The bloodied portions of sand had been hauled out and replaced. Stumpy and Josiah spent the day weaving mats of palm fronds, then placed them on the floor for a modicum of comfort. Others had fashioned a roof from the largest pieces of canvas that they could scrounge. But there was no way yet to make a door to close the front opening and the tabby needed to cure to be fully solid. Still, there would be some protection. The gunner, finally out of misery about midday, had been placed at a safe distance from the encampment and would be buried in the morning INTACT, they hoped.

Beanpole and Jacko were left on watch just outside, on each side of the door. Beanpole kept whining in his grating, high-pitched voice about how hungry he was. He complained about being made to stand watch. He protested about how unfair it was after hauling rock and shell all day. Jacko was not particularly peckish, but relished the thought of how he might first rip out the prattling pest's tongue and eat that first followed by his eyeballs and then all the rest. Even without his tongue, the wretch could still wail. Jacko found that he was, indeed, getting hungry. Soon there was silence.

In the morning, Jacko woke them all to search for Beanpole. They searched through moderate rain, the kind that carries with it a smoky overcast sky and lasts the whole day, but abandoned the effort as the downpour increased. Thankfully, the roof dripped very little. Food must be found soon. Not a single pig had been spotted since that first. It was time to fashion some kind of net. They didn't have enough line and precious little canvas. Josiah suggested making a long basket of palm fronds with a wide weave. They could use it to seine the surf for fish and crabs. When the downpour decreased, Andrew assigned each the task of gathering fronds or weaving the seine.

Somehow, engrossed in the tasks at hand and with weather still pinging the canvas, they forgot about the gunner and Beanpole. At least until Greeby remembered with great shock and remorse, when he almost tripped over the two bodies that had been dragged partially into the brush. The gunner devoid the functions of his brain for many days, was now devoid of his whole head. Beanpole had lost a good fourteen inches off his ungainly height with the loss of his head. Death now part of the daily routine, Greeby continued to gather fronds and informed Andrew when he returned with his load. Andrew decided not to bring up the topic until after the evening meal.

It was a fine feast of freshly caught fish. When everyone was sated, Andrew called for their attention and told them about Greeby's unfortunate discovery. A pall fell over them; no one spoke for some time. They were dumbfounded with fear, for they knew with great certainty that it was not over. There was no further conversation. There was no point. They automatically cleared away the dinner trappings and went silently to their sleeping positions. McGinty and Patel were on for the dog watch. Patel's eyes darted from side to side nervously as he tried to keep his hands from trembling and dropping the spear he held. McGinty chewed on the inside of his lips with wariness. One hour passed, two hours passed, then three. The night dragged on. The two at watch were not the only ones who did not sleep...

The creature had been awakened somehow. A heralding of alien thought invaded the convolutions of its twisted, peaceful, sleeping mind. How *delicious* it was to share similar thoughts! It rose weary and annoyed, but then angry and hungry, very hungry. Driven by primitive thoughts of starvation and clamoring confusion, it was drawn by the smell, thick and coppery, rich and inviting that summoned it relentlessly toward the shore.

It arrived just as the sun melted down into the sea. It was ravenous. Without pause, it devoured the first three heads. They were not fresh, no soft and tasty eyes, just roundish nuggets drying in the sockets, but it didn't matter — a banquet for the taking. The congealing blood dripped from the tips of its pointed, irregular teeth. Brownish red matter the consistency of mud collected at the edges of its malodorous mouth and fell to make little gullies in the sand. More hunger — two more heads. Pause and listen for more thoughts. It was maddening! The external notions burrowed into its brain and fueled its insatiability. The last two heads — rip and gobble. There were no more. The thing wailed and moaned in misery, but went unheard by the ears of the sleeping crew that first night.

For five days it followed them as the sun shined and the rain fell. It tried to communicate with the man who shared its thoughts. The need was overpowering. The sun set on the fifth day and the island was covered in darkness without moon, without stars.

The creature crept up stealthfully to McGinty's left side and snapped his neck, making only a slightly audible sound akin to crushing two paper-shell pecans inside a closed hand. Patel's eyes darted toward McGinty and he turned just in time for a long curved claw to slit his throat, blood and air bubbled through the opening. The creature grabbed each of them by the neck before they hit the ground. It dragged them into the brush a fair distance to feed. This time driven by hunger but also by pleasure, it could take time lingering over each bite — each different taste. It relished the saltiness of the brow and forehead, the texture of the tongue, the softness of the lips, the slipperiness of the brain, and the pop of each eyeball. It slaked its thirst as it slurped the blood. It ate each of the two heads in turn and left the bodies to rot. But the meal only served to multiply its lust for more.

It needed. It hungered. It ran back to the hut drawn by need and hunger. It waited outside the door and whispered a tenuous invitation. Jacko understood and accepted.

The awakened beast heard the blood pumping through the veins of the men. It smelled the flesh. It could sense that they were all fully awake. It salivated as each of them inhaled and exhaled more quickly, as their hearts raced and the adrenaline flowed freely. And now it could smell the fear. Jacko became wild. Infused with the need and the hunger, his eyes bulged and his head pounded as he pushed each of his shipmates out the door — some screaming, some too petrified to make a sound. The creature quickly and deftly dispatched all five of them. In the lack of light, the dead lay in a rising lake of their own bodily fluids.

Jacko and the creature were, indeed, kindred spirits. They shared the echoing shrieks and they partook of the life-force as it ebbed while the blood flowed. Jacko walked expectantly through the opening that would never have a door. He looked forward to a meal well met. And he was.

The Water Witch

Thunder rolled in the distance. It made every impulse of her reckoning whirl with anticipation. The clouds began to race relentlessly across the sky and the wind carried with it the heady fragrance of the storm. She could feel the drops coalescing as they grew into the torrent that approached. For a while, she relaxed on the screen-porch and sipped some fresh-made lemonade. She drew pictograms in the condensation that formed so heavily on the glass. To the uninitiated, it appeared to be meaningless scribbles, but it was all part of what had come to be the ritual. The eves of what once was a handsome little cottage sagged. The stairs up to the porch were bent and broken even though they had not felt the weight of a human footstep in several lifetimes.

Finally, the wind reached down from the clouds and forced the trees to dance in ancient, frantic choreography. Around and around, they circled and arched and bent and bowed. The swirling soil lifted from the dry riverbed to meet the leaves. It was the same dust that scurried around the floor of the cabin and covered the windows and walls in a fine powder of clay and loam. "Soon, soon," she chanted in a voice that sound like the splashing of tiny raindrops. This time, this time it would work!

Everyone knew she could bring the rain. Even when she was very young, barely old enough to walk, and a storm seemed to be approaching, she would wrestle herself from the safety of her mother's care and make her way as fast as she could out into the open. Then she would raise her arms to the sky to join the trees in their frenzied motion, her voice beckoning the much needed rain. And the rain would come. Rain to fill the river, rain to raise the crops, rain to paint the landscape in hues of vibrant green. Throughout the countryside, they remarked that it was good to have a water witch among them. Sometimes they would bring her family extra edibles from their gardens. She especially liked the jams and occasional cakes.

It was time. She set down her glass and ran so quickly and lightly through the door and down the steps, that not even a small speck of dust was disturbed. Under the gnarled and reaching arms of the oaks she moved to the music of the whistling wind with the trees, her willing partners. She longed to face the fury of the storm, but even as her arms stretched up to touch the angry clouds and draw the water from them, the clouds turned quickly to follow a different path. And there was no rain. In eerie silence the trees and the earth cried without tears because they had no moisture with which to make them.

Suddenly, her consciousness transformed her — she was a lovely young girl who laughed and giggled as the rain misted and then ran hard on her face and down her back and onto the ground to create rivulets that sank quickly into the needy soil. The people shared her great joy and followed her lead. Once again a miracle! They all loved her. They were all as children when the ground grew moist and the river swelled. But, one by one, they each stopped their revelry, and stood as still as the stones, that, here and there, lined the riverbed. For now, all of those stones were covered well beyond their depth, but lightening still sizzled and blazed. Nearby, a dancing oak was spit asunder to the explosion of the thunder and the clouds continued to cover the blue that waited on the other side, and the water fell on and on and on. The river, once the beneficent sustainer or life, crept ever closer to its banks like some medieval monster stalking its prey. It was a monster, drooling over the edge of its banks, then lunging and lashing, pouring and pushing its way, inundating, destroying everything in its path.

People were no longer fixed to the ground. They grabbed their sons and daughters and husbands and wives and friends and ran as fast as they could away from the advancing leviathan. Her parents called to her in desperation, but they were not able to reach her in time. She was too close to the river — still dancing with out-stretched arms, her eyes looking to the heavens when she was engulfed and swept away. Her voice of tiny raindrops blended with the sound of the rain itself. The rain finally stopped. And it never rained again in that place because there was no water witch. The years passed, the people moved away, and the homes fell to ruin.

Thunder rolled in the distance. The clouds began to race relentlessly across the sky and the wind carried with it the heady fragrance of the storm. For a while, she relaxed on the screen-porch and sipped some fresh-made lemonade. She drew pictograms in the condensation that formed so heavily on the glass. To the uninitiated it appeared to be meaningless scribbles, but it was all part of what had come to be the ritual. It seemed to her that this was not the first time, but maybe it was. The young girl waited patiently for her family to come home.

The thunder roared as a mighty lion proclaiming its dominion over the storm. She would tame it! The lion's breath stirred the trees. It was time. She set down her glass and ran so quickly and lightly through the door and down the steps, that not even a small speck of dust was disturbed. Instead of wrestling the great beast, she sang to it of the beauty of the flowers and the green of the leaves, and stroked it as if it was the soft, luxurious moss that grew along the river bank. The lion was so moved that it started to cry, and a single tear fell upon her face and ran down her back to join the shimmering streams of water that grew as the raindrops embraced each other, and when the last drop fell, the storm disappeared into the atmosphere as all storms eventually do, and so, finally, did she.

The Little Mermaid

*An original adaptation of the fairytale
as told by Hans Christian Anderson*

She hung there, suspended, immobile. She had
no thoughts and time stood still within her and
the clock ticked in silence. How was it that these
strings confined her mind and rendered her soul
so still? Hapless and helpless and hanging; how
had it come to this? Her eyelids were sealed shut
with the salt that tried to seep through the swollen
slits that had once revealed bright blue, wide-eyed
wonder — eyes that had once looked out at the
world. Then she heard it — a sound smaller than
the weight of a snowflake on the wind. For a long
time it played upon her ear like a memory that she
could not quite recall. She felt impatient when it
became neither louder nor faded away. How im-
pertinent; that almost imperceptible sound! Her
senses yawned and her mind began to stretch for

the first time since — since — when? She tried to suppress the changes, sure that they would worm their way into her universe. The light penetrated just as sharply as a needle. She could not bear it. The dreadful din crowded out the peace that once was and the walls engulfed her, pressing hard on her unwilling flesh — and she was born — sixth in a long line of sisters each, one year older than the other — a daughter of the sea.

The little mermaid began, even at first, to move in close rhythm with the ever undulating pulsing of the waves, eddies, and the tides. Her sisters showed her the wonders of the deep and the blue in her eyes came to reflect the subtle shades that revealed the temperament of the quixotic ocean, the ocean that was, at once, her school and her playground, her protector and her peril. For eons, the small spawn of the coral had lived and died and contributed their skeletons to the colossus that was the reef. When she was young, she knew that there could be nothing so grand, nothing so widely beautiful and mysterious — except, for the sea, itself. Her eyes beheld the mutable landscape as she swam freely through the caverns of coral with current generations vibrating brilliantly in red, orange, yellow, green, blue, indigo, and violet joining in the intricate, eternal patterns of their kind. She took care not to come too close to the eels as they lurked in deep depressions awaiting a meal. She smiled shyly at the color of the comical clowns as they rested easily in the deceptively delicate mouths of the anemones and harvested the leftover crumbs. Sometimes she would dance with the soft sponges as they bowed and arched with the current. It was a world of wonder and innocence, what more could she ever want?

It became time for her eldest sister, who had just turned fifteen, to make her first trip to the surface. The existence of a world other than the one she knew had never been part of the little mermaid's consciousness. Because she was not close in age to that sister, she paid little attention or credence to her sister's rite of passage or to the tales her sister told upon her return. Instead, the young one was content in her wanderings and did not notice that a full year of days and nights had come and gone.

It was time for the next sister to go to the surface, but, still, the little mermaid put it out of her mind. When, in the next year, her third sister returned, she listened to the recounting of the trip, but found the telling so fantastic that she thought it was an elaborate story that her older sisters had spun.

As the next year unfolded, the little mermaid found herself becoming curious about the surface. Could another world actually exist? Her thoughts turned inward to wild imaginings about crossing the barrier between the worlds. She envisioned the surface and it filled her with a strange, new longing that felt like the slow shock of an eel as it traveled through her body downwards from the pit of her stomach all the way to the small scales at the

tip of her tail. She closed her eyes and let the feeling wash over her. She had begun to notice that not
all Merfolk were female. It was worrying.

When her sister, who was just a year older, made
her journey, the little mermaid listened with rapt
attention to the entrancing tales of the humans
who had no tails but moved about on two limbs
and breathed and lived in a place where there was
no water. She could not fathom how this was possible but marveled at her sister's description of the
air that flowed in the way of the water, but was
not water; of how the plants of the air danced like
the soft sponges, and where kelp-like plants grew
tall and thick on mountains of coral that had long-
since been abandoned by the sea.

And, finally, it was her time. Her Father, the
King of the Sea, gave her a protective kiss on her
porcelain cheek, and her ancient grandmother
placed a hei of white flowers atop her long and
golden hair. Her sisters hugged her as if it would be
the last time they would be able. They each knew
that, even though she would come back, her passage would be solitary and changing.

It was the beginning of day as she broke the barrier. She waited on the water and watched the sun
beginning its climb from the edge of the horizon in
ruby-colored robes. The reflection reached across
the sea to touch her gently with a delicate blush.
So fascinated was the little mermaid with the play
of light, that she did not see the ship that lay becalmed in anticipation of the morning breeze. As

the sun trekked higher, it shed its robes to reveal golden rays that matched the mermaid's hair as it bounced off her tresses. When the current brought her closer, she could not help but notice the ship. It was fortunate that her hair and the blue-green of her tail blended with the sea. She scanned the ship. Her eyes traveled along the planks and up to the portside rail. And then she saw him — he had a more comely face than any she had ever imagined. His dark short curls hung saucily down to his neck and moved slightly in the now building breeze. She shuddered slightly when he turned his deep sea-green eyes in her direction, but he did not see her. As he came closer to the bow she was startled when she saw that he had no tail. She turned away, dismayed, but then she turned back and watched, fascinated, as he purposefully, yet gracefully, stepped forward on his muscular legs. And now, she could not take her eyes from him. She swam to and fro darting from stem to stern, side to side to make sure that she did not lose sight of him. She was frantic when he disappeared below. She had to swim very fast to keep pace after they set the sails and caught the ever increasing wind.

The clouds first appeared as small playful tufts of sea foam, but they quickly changed into huge, dark, riling, fighting serpents hurling flashing spears. One could hear and feel the sound of the battle in the once silent sea where the mountains of water angrily tossed and finally crushed the foundering ship. This done, the storm had played itself out. All was blackness.

She sang sweetly, in her clear and perfect voice to draw him to her, but he did not come. She searched among the bits of wreckage that floated aimlessly, but he was not there. She looked toward the close by land where the tempest had driven them, but to no avail. She dove deep down into her realm and there she found him. She cradled him tightly in her arms and made her way up hoping that he would be able to breathe anew when they reached the surface, but he did not. Holding him tightly to her bosom, she brought him to the shore where she laid him gently with his head elevated on a pile of weed that washed in during the night. But still, he drew no air. She placed her lips upon his and in great passion imparted some of her life force. His chest heaved, the saltwater escaped through his mouth, and he drew a breath. He lived!

She saw a mighty temple upon the cliff and hoped that someone would see him. Reluctantly, she swam out a small distance hoping for help. In a while, a group of girls came down the steep steps toward the beach. One of them spotted him, ran to him, and knelt beside him. It was at this moment that he awoke to see the young priestess, his salvation. The young man, a prince, as it so happens, was nursed to health by this maiden and, afterward, returned to his homeland knowing that she was his true Love. The mermaid, a princess, returned to her home knowing that the young man was her true Love.

Time passed; the mermaid was obsessed. She asked everyone she knew and everyone they knew if they would help her find him. She asked the fish and the whales and the seabirds. She searched the shoreline. One day, there he was, in a palace by the sea leaning over the balcony just as she had seen him leaning over the rail that day on the ship. And, once again, she felt the electricity travel through her. She must become human, even though it would shorten her lifetime. Better to have fifty years in his arms than three hundred in the claws of the cursed sea!

In desperation, she made her way through the dead zone in the dark, dangerous, depths — where the coral was brittle and colorless, where no sea fans fluttered, no kelp flourished, no fish swam, and even the eels dared not to go. It was the place of the sea witch. When the mermaid saw the sorceress, her own beating heart seemed to freeze and she could not breathe. The witch's skin lacked any color, it was difficult to discern the exact shape or nature of her form, and her piercing eyes were devoid of any kindness or mercy or love; they were endless emptiness. The witch knew why the mermaid had come and offered her a potion that would transform the young mermaid's elegant tale into two lovely legs so that she might walk as a human on the land and win the heart of her prince. The mermaid accepted the potion and held it carefully in her trembling hand. Why, it was so easy! She chastened herself for not coming to the witch sooner. She made her thanks and turned to swim away, anxious to find her Love, but she did not make more than three strokes of her tail when the wicked one called her back to tell her the true price of the potion.

The mermaid would, indeed, walk upon the land, but each step would carry with it the pain of walking on the small sharp blades of many knives. As she drank it, the mixture, itself, would send the searing pain of a sword as if she was being carved from the inside out. This, she could endure, but then she heard the last and most dear. The witch would cut out and keep the mermaid's tongue, for she coveted the pure and perfect voice of the young princess. The clever witch convinced the little mermaid that her love was so strong that she could win the prince without words or song. And — there was another codicil. She would never be able to return to the sea. And should she not be able to do so before he wed another, the mermaid would cease to exist as if she had never been born. Her father and grandmother and sisters were heart-sore and mourned even before she departed. Never again would they be warmed by her smile or transported by her magical voice. They warned and begged her not to go, but who where they to tell her not to follow her heart? As she swam swiftly toward the shore, they sang sweetly to her and implored her to return with them beneath the waves. But the wind carried their songs away from the shore far out to sea and she did not hear them.

With great effort, she pulled herself through the rocks close to shallows near the tidal pools at a place just beneath the palace and, there, she swallowed the dark draught. It sliced down her throat and cut through her body with every heartbeat. The skin of her tail ripped apart and the shining scales were strewn to the seven seas. Waves took the skin from the shore where sharks fell upon it in frenzy. The pain forced tears from her eyes and shrieked so loudly in her ears that blood dripped from them. As the full moon rose and she beheld her two human legs. She swooned and fell unconscious.

It was the custom of the Prince to stroll upon the strand at the first light. And there he saw her, stretched upon the rocks. He marveled at her beauty and her innocence. The sight awoke a desire in him and he remembered the forbidden priestess. The little mermaid with her new-found human appearance lay there protected only by an occasional lock of golden, flowing hair. He wrapped his cloak around her as he lifted her slight form into his arms and carried her to his home where ladies tended to her.

The Prince was impatient to talk with her, to hear the pure, perfect voice he sensed she must possess. But when, he spoke and questioned her, she was silent, and he wept to see that her tongue had been torn out. In loss, they came to share many things. They rode and fished and hunted. She slept on a soft sleek velvet sofa not far from his door and

became his Page, for his father would not toler-
ate his son's request to marry her — a foundling
so far beneath a Prince's station! And she would
have done so even knowing that the Prince could
never forget the one who he thought had rescued
him from the edge of the sea. She had no voice to
tell him that it was, she, herself, who saved him
from the icy fingers of death. She had no voice to
tell him that she was a Princess. Sometimes they
would dance, their bodies in liquid symmetry. It
reminded her a bit of the soft sponges and of her
family somewhere in the briny blue. From time to
time she tasted home in her own tears.

The Prince fought desperately against his be-
trothal to a princess he had never met from a land
far away that he had never seen, but there was
nothing to be done about it. As the wedding day
approached, he planned an escape with his darling
Page, but, of course, it never happened. The mermaid knew that if another became his bride, she
would cease; no part or thought or memory of her
would remain.

The news of the impending royal marriage
spread across the land and even down into the
depths of the ocean. The couple was to be joined at
the time of the new moon, and when they met he
saw that she was not a stranger, but, instead, his
true Love who had only been a student at the temple. They rejoiced in reunion and exchanged vows.

On that same night, five sisters swam to the
shore beneath the palace balcony and sang in a

language that they knew their youngest sibling would recognize. She walked across the sand and found them perched upon the rocks, their wretched, close-cropped hair almost hidden in the lack of light. They had traded it to the sea witch for a magical knife that they then handed to her and told her how her beloved could now save *her* life — all she had to do was slit *his* throat.

With the weight of death she slipped, stealthily into the bridal chamber, softly stepping toward the bower. The lantern shone a shaft of soft light on the faces of the newlyweds as they lay entwined in the deep repose of new love — and she could not lift the blade. She knew then, that there was no sacrifice that true love would not bear.

She found herself at the shimmering shore where the phosphorescent foam jumped from layer to layer of incoming water and prepared to face oblivion. But as her toes touched the sea, she found that she did not end. Instead, she became a part of the eternal, endless ocean. The ocean that turns and tumbles and travels all places on the earth and melts into the air and falls as droplets upon the thirsty soil and then rejoins the sea in a never ending song waiting to be reborn — this time a daughter of the land.

The Lighthouse Keeper's Wish

He knew he had to light the light. It was his job, after all. But he also knew that they were drawn to it like moths to a flame — no — as if it was the light that one follows at the end of days. They didn't always come, only on overcast or rainy nights or at the dark of the moon. Maybe they were confused and lost just trying to find their way home. He supposed that on brighter nights they probably chased the shining path on the water trying to get to the moon. He never saw or felt or heard them on those nights. Well, it wasn't that he really ever heard them. It was a sort of vibration that chilled him to his very bones and made every hair on his body stand at attention.

His friends thought that he was crazy to take a job in such a lonely, isolated, god-forsaken place, but he still wanted to be close to the water. He missed his days on the tall ships. He missed the sunrises and sunsets and the mist, and knowing he was almost home when he saw the light.

He shuddered as he ignited the oil, *there will be no moon tonight.* Immediately, the light became magnified and broken and sent out across the water, a beacon to shine through the night and the storm and even down into the depths.

They could float, you know. They could float through the water or on the air, spirits of so little substance, yet too heavy to dissipate upon the wind. Sometimes they could be seen gathering close to the light, trying to touch it, yet somehow never being able to penetrate the outside glass. But it was *her* eyes that kept him from just extinguishing the flame and locking the door and never coming back.

Unlike the others, she was not so transfixed upon the flame; she looked straight at him, her hands upraised as if to lean against the glass and peer in. Her eyes bore into him with a loneliness that burned his heart — branded it. He wanted so to ease her pain; it became his pain. He wished that there was some way that he could help her. Each dawn as they moved out of sight, he was riddled with remorse.

Souls from the deep, innocents lost to the storm—borne down by the icy claws of the deep as the waves washed 'round—lost, as they were trapped below or pinned on deck by broken bits of the rig. Gasping their last as the water rushed into their lungs, they fought so hard to live that they did not realize they had died.

She did not seem to be so confused. Night after night she would appear; time after time she would be drawn to the light as were the others, and then give all her attention to him. Oh, she had been so beautiful — long raven hair, lithe of body! Then, it happened; her outstretched arm passed through the glass and touched his cheek. The chill was gone, replaced by the heat of love. But the loneliness and, now, longing was still to be seen in her clear, blue, unwavering eyes.

On bright nights he was restless and could not sleep. On dark nights, he waited long after twilight, until she came—and he did not sleep. Night after night, he waited. So great was his need to see her, so great was her sorrow that he could scarcely eat or sleep or breathe until she returned.

He became so gaunt of face and sunken in the eyes that when he went into town to get supplies, people began to stare at him and inquire after his health, but it did not matter. *She* was all that mattered. Finally, he got tired of the questions and stopped going into town.

It was a moonless night. He so longed to see her. He used the door to the outside walkway that circumferenced the large glass windows at the top of the building. The light blazed at his back so that any on-looker would have seen him only as a silhouette. It was November and the wind blew high signaling the impending winter. He could smell and hear the waves below as they crashed against the rocks, at the bottom of the lighthouse, and along the jetty. He waited.

They came. *She* came. She looked into his eyes and for the first time he saw joy in them and a gentle smile graced her lips. She beckoned to him and he stepped off the walkway into her outstretched arms. He felt the heat, and he felt the rocks. And he knew that she was alone no more.

The Third Knot

Inspired by a traditional Finnish legend of a magic rope that can be used to capture the wind.

From the time that they were young children and played hide-and-seek in and around the small fishing boats and the nets as they hung to dry, Ilma and Sisu were destined to become husband and wife.

A diminutive girl with wispy, almost transparent silver-blond hair, Ilma, appeared as if she could be carried away by the slightest gust of wind. This was fitting, perhaps, as she was named after the air. It was her nature to move quickly without thinking, to change her direction (and mind) as quixotically as the wind, and to allow her curiosity to take her to places she should not go. It suffered her parents to worry about their only child both day and night. They hoped that she would be become more cautious and learn to control her tongue as she matured. At play, she would taunt Sisu mercilessly when he did not find her fast enough, "You search like a snail." or she would snigger and say, "Must I always jump up to show you where I am?" Sisu would just walk up to her with a smile and do what he always did to stop her. He would lift her at the waist and hold her above his head while she squirmed, "How will you run and hide if I refuse to let you go?" It was not as if Sisu did not make a bit of mischief of his own.

From the time that he was born, Sisu showed the willpower, determination, and strength that his name signified. Even as a boy, he contemplated the meaning of each new word as he learned it and measured the weight of each word that he uttered. His parents knew that his resourcefulness would only grow with time and gave him great encouragement in his endeavors. Because of his size and composure, he was allowed to accompany his father on short fishing trips at a younger age than most of the other boys. He would help to set the big weirs on the river during the salmon run and thrilled to the grace of the fish as they danced in the net. And he ate them with reverence when he recalled their dance. He tried to describe it to Ilma, "Their forms were slippery, shiny crescents that arched and reeled and wiggled. Sparks seemed to fly as the sunlight bounced from their scales!" She listening as she ate each tasty morsel of the fish but could not envision the dance. She was at least wise enough, though, not to tell him so. But his poetry began to hold more meaning for her as she reached puberty, when his voice took a lower tone and she finally began to understand the passion behind his words. It was only then that she began to look at him as more than a childhood friend. She began to watch him often from the corners of her almost almond shaped, sea-green eyes.

From time to time, they would accompany each other to the edge of the nearby lake where they would fish with wooden lures to catch pike and perch. Their families would have a common meal. The women and older girls, Ilma, now included, cleaned the catch and smoked the fish over a slow fire surrounded by stones. There was homemade dark rye bread and mushrooms seasoned with dill and onion. And there were fresh lingonberries for dessert. Sisu and Ilma caught just the right amount of fish to fill each happy stomach. It was full dark and time to share the old poems of Kalevala. Because they had provided the feast, the two were honored to be able the start the song in alternating lines about the creation from a duck egg and first man. Their voices paired well in the alliteration and meter. Others picked up when the young ones came to the end of what they had learned. The telling of the first cycle continued. They heard of Aino drowning herself in the sea and of the forging of the Sampo. The ballad went long into the night. The youngest of the children had long since fallen into slumber without hearing the end. Those who were a bit older listened with rapt attention until, they too, no matter how hard they tried, could not keep from closing their eyes and falling into a deep sleep. But Sisu and Ilma reveled in the songs and shared every emotional turn brought about by the telling. Through it all, they held hands.

It could not have been a week later that Sisu told her that he would be going to sea. His dream was to work the commercial fishing boats and make enough money to be able to build one of his own. "How could you not tell me of this dream? How could you leave me? You are always so selfish." Ilma was livid. His motivation was anything but selfish, of course. His dream was to care for her and make a boat for just the two of them so they could always be together. She stomped away and closed her ears. He stood, unable to move.

"But I do this for us, I...I love you." Sisu, the young man of great strength, started to shed one tear after another and called after her as he followed, "Ilma, Ilma..." He felt as if he was an abandoned child searching her out among the little boats and hanging nets. But he could not find her. He waited for her to jump up and call him names and chide him for his slowness, but she did not. Neither would she see him in any of the remaining days before his departure. And it was too late when she finally relented.

She walked along the shore and looked out into the endless ocean trying to see his ship. It just wasn't fair! Sometimes she thought she would drown herself like Aino. It would serve him right! She kicked the sand and smashed several small shells with her heels. Once again, her parents began to worry after her. It was not unusual that she still shirked some her chores as if she was still a child, but after a while she would not bother to come home until after the moon rose, and many times, slept fitfully without eating an evening meal. Ilma began to look almost as wispy as her hair. The color faded from the hollows of what were once soft, rosy, rounded cheeks. She hummed the ancient poems to herself watching the water fill the little depressions left by her heels in the sand. Her parents longed to hear her thoughtlessly comment about anything, but she just hummed and soon made no sounds at all. One misty evening after many, many months she did not return.

It was two years to the day that Sisu left when the letter came. He would be home with his newly built fishing sloop in the spring just as the berries were about to bloom! Her parents read the letter and prayed that she would finally return. The berry bushes were sprinkled with the white blossoms when he knocked at their door. When it opened his face colored with the anticipation of seeing her once again and finally holding her in his arms. He was greeted with great welcome and caring by her parents. They invited him to sit in at the table in the chair closest the fire because the full chill of winter was not yet completely gone and the clouds were building. A cup of hot tea and a small glass of pontikka were placed on the table for each of them. Ilma was noticeably missing. Holding back tears until it was impossible, her mother spoke in a paper-thin voice to Sisu. The rain drummed a death beat on the roof. His face was now the color of bleached cowry shells. The deafening din of the rain pounded above them and poured down the sides of the small cottage. The woman sobbed. Her husband held her trembling shoulders as salty droplets dripped from his own eyes. Sisu wrenched himself from the chair, opened the front door, closed it softly behind himself and walked out into the torrent of a pitch-black night.

The cold rain pressed his clothing tight to his skin. His boots were sucked down into the sand each time he stepped and the waves pulled the water away, but he kept on and on and on. The warmth of the cottage drained from him as he walked, minute by minute, hour by hour. Light did not come easily to the new day; the clouds were suspended, steel gray, and continued to spit lightly on the earth below. He could feel it rolling down the back of his neck. The water lapped at his soles. His body was absent heat except for the smallest spark to keep him alive. Without essential heat, every muscle in his body was board-stiff and almost beyond control. Breath did not come easily to him. He turned his head slightly to one side and scanned the beach. He did not know where he was and screamed as loudly as he could, "Where am I?" But it was only a whisper. He was sure that he was past the possibility of survival and spoke her name, "Ilma, my lo...?" His voice was not loud enough anymore to be a whisper.

He awakened on the other side. An unearthly light shone from the walls of a seemingly great cave. Somehow he knew that she would be there — and she was! But he was not dead. And *she* was not dead. Confusion claimed his mind. He could see her, older and...different. Her hair was braided elaborately and decorated with small shells, her still slight but now womanly attributes were hidden only minimally by the remains of what had been a dress and adorned with kelp. She radiated heat so strongly that the pain and stiffness of his limbs subsided. "You have returned. I hoped that you would. I waited." Her speech was hesitant as one who has not spoken for a very long time. She bent close to him and peered into his eyes. He searched in hers to find Ilma. He saw her as she had always been, a lovely selfish, delightful child.

"How is this possible?" His voice was almost inaudible. She did not answer. He did not care. There were both here, alive. "But it makes no sense," his mind answered. *"Reason be damned!"* He was beyond rationale thought. What did it matter that she had, as usual, won the game of hide-and-seek. He took her hand and led her from the cave across the lowest tide into the bright golden light of early day. They walked down the beach until the stars returned to a clear spring sky. They walked until they came to the dimly lighted cottage and knocked on the door. Her father caught his wife whose legs buckled under the weight of such happiness.

A heavy log was set on the fire. There was tea and pontikka, dark bread and smoked salmon with lingonberry jam. There were smiles and sighs and tears of joy, but for most of the day there was no need for words. At sunset, it was her mother that finally broke the silence, "My precious daughter, why did you not come home? Where were you? What happened?"

"Aiti, I do not remember."

"But you must remember something!"

"Only walking along the sand and into the water. That is all."

Her mother looked deep into her daughter's innocent eyes of green and saw there what she had always seen, a lovely selfish, delightful child. No one asked again and no one wondered. What did it matter? There were no more questions. There were no more doubts, there was no more waiting. The two who had been meant for each other made preparations to wed. But now and again, Ilma would dream of languishing in the cave. She saw snippets of strange and beautiful creatures that were almost as light as the air and mutable as the foam. Somehow she knew that they had saved her body from staving and helped her remember her sanity when they led Sisu to her. But all recollection of those events vanished each time she awoke.

There could be no marriage without a celebration. It was a celebration greater than perhaps any the village had ever had. After all, it was also a homecoming! Preparations were rushed and took only one week. The fishermen set the weir on the river to catch the salmon. Sisu helped. It was good to be home. Children gathered wild mushrooms with the watchful mentoring of the elderwoman. Boys and girls fished the lake for pike and perch with wooden lures. Women baked dark bread. Dried berries were mixed with barley to add to a fish stew. They would not only be providing the food for the feast which would last all day and into the next, but provisions for the coupling voyage on Sisu's new sloop, *Meri*, named to honor the sea upon which she sailed.

Ilma's mother took her wedding dress, the dress that had belonged to her mother, and her mother's mother. Her thoughts brought her back to the time went she had the same straw-yellow hair of her brothers and sisters. She thought about them at work and play laughing together, one large happy family — about how their broad smiles as she wore her mother's dress and of how proud and thankful they were for her when Ilma, her only child was born. "What is it?" Ilma asked as she ran quickly to the cottage at her mother's call.

"It is time to fit your dress." The bride to be knew of the dress as it was the custom. But she had never seen it and when her mother held it up to the light of the open window, the sun captured every delicate detail. It glistened with small bits of abalone shell and revealed the complex intricate patterns of embroidery accented here and there with the tiniest of pearls. She was thrilled that it was now hers. It hung large and awkward on her small frame.

"But it is so big. How will it ever fit!" she balked. Her mother assured her that it was easy enough to make it look perfect. Privately, her mother was taken aback. She thought that whatever had happened while her daughter was missing would have made her more mindful of what she said. But the thought came and went quickly, the dress was expertly altered without losing any of the original material, and the eager anticipation of the wonderful event was not dulled.

It was the morning of her wedding day. As was the custom, Ilma took the case that covered her pillow and went to the house of each wedding guest to collect small gifts — a plate here, a cup there, candles and candies, a tin of tea and other such items. When she came to the cozy cottage of the elderwoman, she was invited to come in for a cup of tea. The woman shared the many secrets that a man and a woman held within their love and then walked to a corner of the room and took a single item from the carved chest that was nestled there. It was a small, weathered canvas pouch. The woman placed it into Ilma's hands. The girl's curiosity far outpaced her fearfulness. "I must know what is inside," she demanded! In a voice as old as the wind, the woman instructed the girl to open the pouch and remove its contents.

Why it's an old, knotted bit of rope. What kind

of a wedding gift is that? the girl was not so foolish as to give voice to her thoughts. It was widely understood that the elderwoman was wise in many things, even the singing of magic.

The ancient voice spoke, "Your husband will know how to use this. You may return it to the pouch now."

"But what is it? I need to know," the girl whined.

"Control your curiosity and your tongue. This gift and this advice is given with the best of wishes for your happiness, success, and safety." The perturbed bride extended thanks for the gift, a grudging hug, and went on her way.

The wedding was splendid! Sisu had never seen Ilma look so beautiful and Ilma had never seen Sisu look so handsome. The crowd could feel the energy that passed between the two. Everyone ate and drank and danced and sang stories. When the time came, Ilma removed the golden crown from her head and passed it to the one who would be the next bride. Finally, they danced the last waltz and the couple walked hand in hand sharing a love that seemed to bypass even death. They walked down the pier, boarded the boat and descended the companion way to the small cabin that had been thoughtfully decorated with fragrant flowers. They traded their childhood games and found each other.

As the first rays of sun played upon the ripples in a light breeze, the newlyweds loosed the lines and embarked upon their journey together as man and wife. It was a pleasant spring day as they hugged the shore and talked of Sisu's adventures when he was abroad. The *Meri* proved yar even to the unfamiliar hand of the new bride. They ate and drank and laughed and loved. Occasionally, they would take a gift from the pillowcase and remark on each one as they recovered it from the bag.

On the second day, when the breeze ceased, they were becalmed, but did not fret. They amused themselves by, once again, dipping into the store of gifts. It was Sisu's turn to drawn a gift this time. He pulled out the small, weathered, canvas bag.

"Oh, that," said Ilma, "It's just an old piece of rope tied in knots! The elderwoman showed it to me on our wedding day. And, can you imagine, she refused to tell me what it was for!"

Ilma prattled on indignantly. But Sisu did not seem to hear her. He looked in wonder at the three knots, and held the bit of line with a reverence and an interest that silenced his young wife.

She squinted the almond shape of her eyes into little slits and burned with curiosity. "Please, please tell me what it is." He declined softly and told her that it was simply a sailor's tool and not to worry about it. She was not happy and went to the bow of the boat and sulked.

He stood aft and secretly untied one of the knots. When he did so, the breeze freshened, wind filled the sails, and they cut the small waves as they glided smoothly a little further from the shore. The cooling wind and movement suited Ilma and put her in a much better mood as she experience the illusion of standing still while the landscape moved in front of her. Sisu stored the rope, now with two knots, back in its pouch under the mattress where it would not tempt his bride. She looked aft to see his coppery hair blaze in the sunlight and stream behind him as he met the wind and the waves almost head-on at a close reach.

That night they dropped anchor in a small cove. It was not safe to sail so close to shore in the now increasing wind. They went below to get out of the chill and warmed each other as they moved to the rhythm of the halyard against the mast. When Ilma fell asleep, Sisu felt for the small pouch under his side of the mattress in the small V berth at the bow. In the dark, he deftly located the line and re-tied the knot that he had loosed earlier, put it back inside the bag, and tucked it under the mattress. In no time at all, the wind calmed down, and the halyard ceased its clanging sound.

Ilma was growing weary of their pace. Day after day it was the same. She wanted excitement. Her husband in an effort to try to please his new bride, decided to head away from the shallows near the shore where he untied two of the knots. Being a fisherman and a sailor, he was schooled in the lore of the sea. His people had known the sea for 10,000 years. He had heard the myths about being able to reef the wind with magic, but he never dared to think it was truly possible. His willpower was strong enough to quell the childish curiosity which with his wife had infected him. He was not quite prepared, though, for the instantaneous increase in the velocity when he untied the second knot. It was thrilling. Ilma came from below and stood facing forward at the top of the ladder steadying herself with a hand on each side of the companionway. It filled her with awe and exhilaration. She wanted more. She always wanted more...and she had seen Sisu loose the knots. And she now knew the power that was held in that frayed and frazzled bit of line. She was curious about what would happen if she undid the third knot.

Ilma begged to take the helm. They stood together holding the tiller side by side, and felt the rush of the wind and power of the waves in their hands. Sisu closed his eyes for a few moments just to drink in the feeling. Ilma carefully removed the rope from his pocket where he had tucked it away. She worked the last knot free. The wind roared and pushed with such force that the small craft began heeling dangerously to port. As Sisu grabbed desperately for the mainsheet he saw that Ilma held the magic line in her tiny hand. It was being whipped by the wind and held not a single knot. In an instant he realized what had happened. He had lost their final game of hide-and-seek. Overpowered, the *Meri*, despite her namesake, was no match for the white squall.

Everyone waited for the couple to return. Any day now they would see the sloop making its course along the shore. They would greet them with a hardy welcome. The sailors would make it through the storm and come safely home —but they never did.

The storm raged for many days. During a short lull, the elderwoman walked down to the shore and examined the flotsam that had washed up upon the beach. She retrieved a bit of ragged rope, shook her head, shed a single tear, neatly tied three evenly spaced knots in the small length of line, and placed it into her apron. With that, the wind and sea laid down and slept.

Even today, the people of that village will tell you to go down to the place on the shore where the old woman reclaimed the rope. They will tell you to open your mind and your ears in the stillness that precedes the storm, when the world is held prisoner in the thickness of the air. It is then that you can hear Ilma and Sisu singing the old stories in tandem, until the whistling of the wind and the heavy hammers of thunder and the relentless roaring of the waves, once again, takes them down into the deepness of sea where they wait impatiently to herald the next storm.

About the Author

As a professional touring musician and story-teller, songsmith, author, artist, and educator, Chris Kastle has performed throughout the United States and in Canada, Europe, and New Zealand. As a recording artist, and part of a duo, she has released twelve critically acclaimed music CDs and a DVD as well as three solo CDs of music and spoken word.

As an educator, she has worked as the Director of Education at the St. Augustine Lighthouse & Museum, an instructor for the Inland Seas Education Association, a Visiting Professor at Governors State University, Community Educator for Friends of A1A Scenic & Historic Coastal Byway, has done a myriad of educational residencies, is currently on the faculty at the Old Town School of Folk Music, and a Teaching Artist for VSAFL (Very Special Arts Florida).

As an author, she has penned articles for maritime publications and been a contributing author in a maritime history anthology published by Lake Claremont Press. She has many original short stories to her credit and is the author/illustrator of the children's book, *Dolly the Decorator Crab*, inspired by her work as a teaching artist for VSAFL.

As a visual artist, Chris has helped students of many ages and abilities to create personal and collaborative artwork such as sculpture, collage, set design, and puppets. Her individual work has been displayed alongside that of her students at the Cummer Museum of Arts and Gardens and by the Thrasher-Horne Center for the Arts.

As an arts administrator, advocate, and producer, she is the Executive Director of Common Times, the folk-arts organization that presents the "Chicago Maritime Festival" and the "Chinquapin Folk Music and Storytelling Festival" and has served on the boards of the Florida Storytelling Association and the Tale Tellers of St. Augustine.

She is a one-time Tall Ship sailor from Chicago who has found a new home in St. Augustine, the nation's oldest port city, enjoying the best of the old world and the new!

Chris can be contacted through her website: www.chriskastle.com.

Other Works by Chris Kastle

Books available at www.chriskastle.com

Dolly The Decorator Crab
A picture book for children

From Lumber Hookers to the Hooligan Fleet: A Treasury of Chicago Maritime History
(Contributor)

Sound recordings available at CDBaby.com
(CD or Download)

Down Below the Waves
Traditional and original maritime songs and stories

Some Here and Some Now
Original songs and personal stories

The Roaring Rhinoceros and Friends
Original songs and stories for children